Magic in the Attic

A Button & SQUEAKY Adventure

JIMSHORE

Happy Fox BOOKS

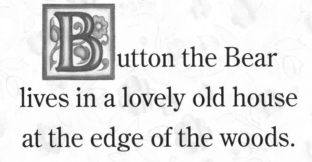

Button the Bear
lives in a lovely old house
at the edge of the woods.

He's happy there and usually very busy.

But sometimes he feels
something's missing . . .

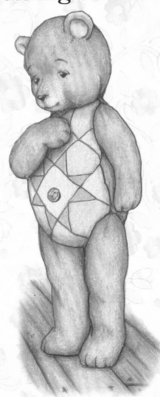

Button looks out the window.
It's a dreary, drizzly day.
He doesn't want to go out in the rain.
He doesn't like it when his fur gets wet.

Button thinks, "I'm a little blue today."

He looks down at his belly.
"Then again, I'm always a little blue."

That makes him smile.

Button shrugs, "I guess it's not that bad.
But I still need something to do!"
Looking around, he sees a key in the attic door.
Button has never been in the attic before.
"Today is the day. I'm going to explore the attic!"

utton gives the key a twist. He hears a click!

He turns the doorknob and with a creaky sound, the door slowly opens.

Button's eyes get wider. "This might just be a real adventure," he whispers to himself.

utton pulls the door all the way
open.

A tall, narrow set of stairs
leads to the attic.

Even though it's dark and scary,
Button says, "I'm going up!"

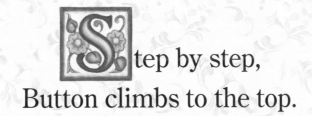

Step by step,
Button climbs to the top.

He peers into the darkness.
What lies beyond the top stair?
He sees a light switch,
"Phew!" and flips it on.

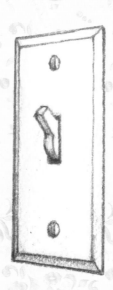

s the darkness fades away,
a wonderland appears.

The attic is filled with all sorts of
mysterious and fantastic things.

Button doesn't know what to
look at first.

There's an Aladdin lamp
and a lighthouse!

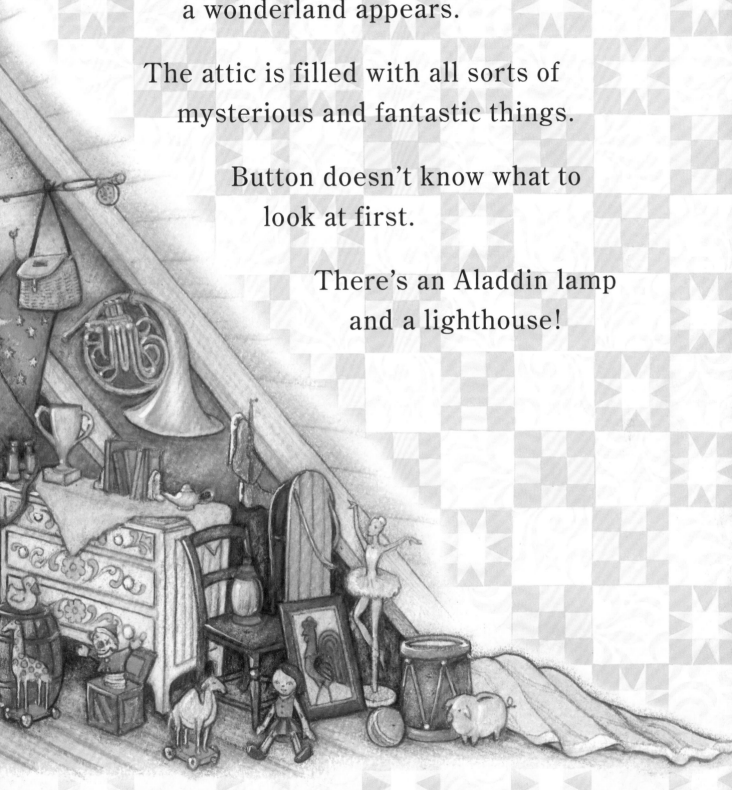

Ahot air balloon and a plane to travel the world.

A globe, to show where a bear is going and where a bear has been.

A fireman's hat that's a little too big.

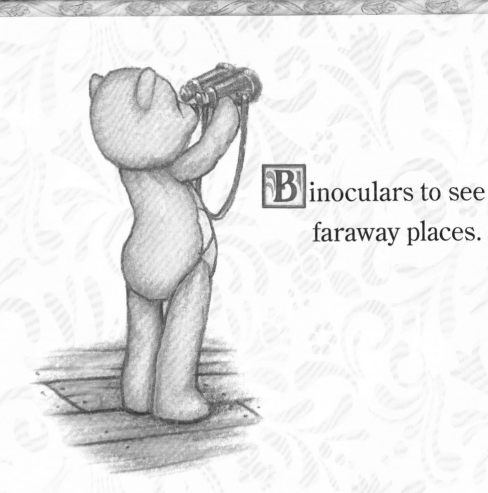

Binoculars to see
faraway places.

Then tea for when
he is tired from
traveling the world.

All of a sudden Button notices a beautiful glow
in a corner of the attic. "It's the trunk!"
he says, "It's glowing!"

The trunk is covered with stickers from all over the
world: Egypt, Paris, Brazil, and many more.
Some of the places he's never even heard of!
He remembers the globe.
Where could all the places be?

"I wonder what's in it? Whatever it is,
I bet it's going to be good!
I'll just take a peek."

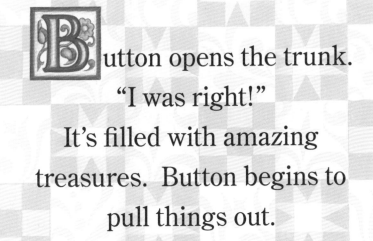

utton opens the trunk.

"I was right!"

It's filled with amazing

treasures. Button begins to

pull things out.

irst a feather boa and glasses and a lovely fan. He puts them on and fans himself, feeling very fancy.

utton tries on the top hat, hoping no bunnies will fall out.

"I could use this old jar for catching fireflies," he says.

Next, he finds a shiny brass spyglass. With it, he could see forever. "Maybe a pirate used this!"

Under the spyglass is a party mask.

"I'll wear this, and no one will know who I am."

own in the deep bottom of the trunk is a little box with a funny picture. A tag on the box says, "Instant Friend, Just Add Love and Air."

"Hmmmmm."

Button opens the little box. Out falls a long purple balloon and a piece of paper.

"What's this?" he asks. "'Instant Friend'?"

"I hope this works. I've always wanted a friend."

Button decides to give it a try.

e blows into the balloon again and again.
"Boy, that sure took a lot of air!"
Then Button goes to work.

queak, twist, squeak . . .
"That's not good."

wist, squeak, twist . . .
"That didn't go well."

Twist, twist, squeak . . .
"Neither did that."

Squeak, squeak, twist . . .
"Whew!"

None of it works.
"Making friends is harder
than I thought," Button says.

"I'm getting nowhere fast," Button says. Then he remembers the piece of paper still lying on the floor.

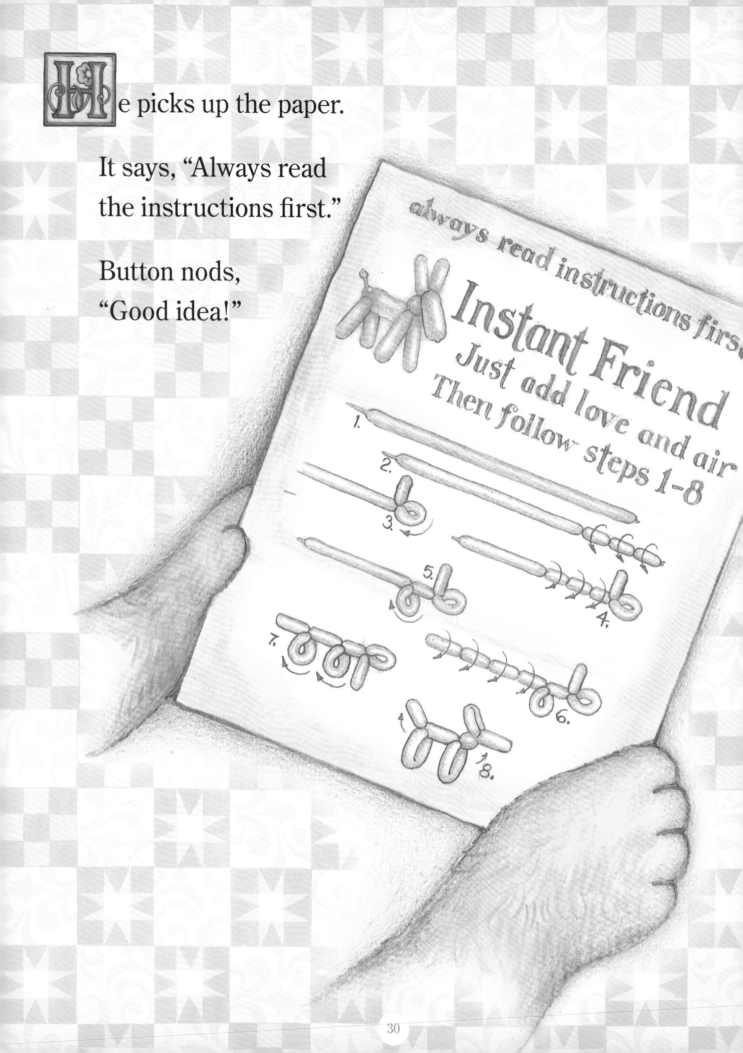

e picks up the paper.

It says, "Always read
the instructions first."

Button nods,
"Good idea!"

always read instructions first

Instant Friend
Just add love and air
Then follow steps 1-8

1.
2.
3.
4.
5.
6.
7.
8.

As Button follows the instructions, something starts to happen. It's almost like magic. Maybe it *is* magic! A creature starts to appear . . . a little purple dog.

Button sets the dog on the floor.

It squeaks and wags its tail!

In front of Button stands a real-life balloon dog.
"I'm Button. What's your name?" he asks.

The balloon dog answers! "I'm Squeaky."

"I know you are, but what's your name?"
Button asks again.

"I'm Squeaky."

"OH!" Button has figured it out.
The dog's name is Squeaky.

Button has made a new friend. Squeaky.

Squeaky says to Button, "Thank you for the air,
but I didn't feel the kind of love that comes
when making a new friend."

Button scratches his nose.
He's not really sure what love is.

Then Squeaky says,
"Wait a minute.
I have something
that might help."

Squeaky jumps back into the trunk.

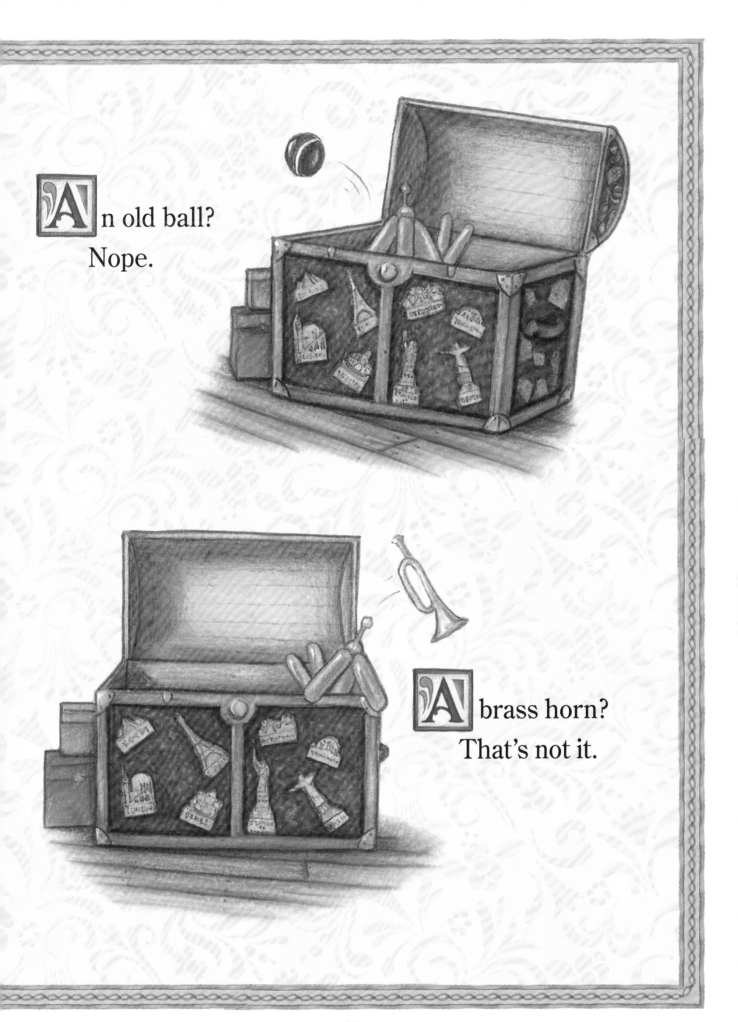

An old ball?
Nope.

A brass horn?
That's not it.

A bell?
It's good for
ringing, but
not for love.

A clock won't do
the trick either.

Just when Button can barely see Squeaky, out jumps the little balloon dog again. "I found it!" Squeaky cries.

beautiful heart made from old fabric
is balanced on Squeaky's nose.

"Button, this heart is for you," Squeaky says.
"But you'll have to sew it on yourself.
I never touch needles."
Squeaky gives a little shudder.

A warm feeling spreads through Button's little body.
He's never been given a present before.

utton remembers seeing an old sewing basket on one side of the attic.

He looks through the basket. Sure enough, he finds a needle and thread. He gets to work.

He pokes the thread through the eye of the needle, then knots the end. He places the heart just where he wants it and begins to stitch. Needle in, needle out, needle in, needle out. Needles don't scare a teddy bear. Not like a balloon dog!

Button sews all the way around the heart. He wants to make sure it will never fall off.

After sewing on his heart,
Button shows Squeaky.

Squeaky agrees, the
heart is perfect!

He wags his little
purple tail.

oday is a day filled with firsts for Button.

His first time in the attic!

His first present!

And best of all, his first friend.

"Making a friend isn't that hard after all,"
Button says. "All you have to do is keep trying."

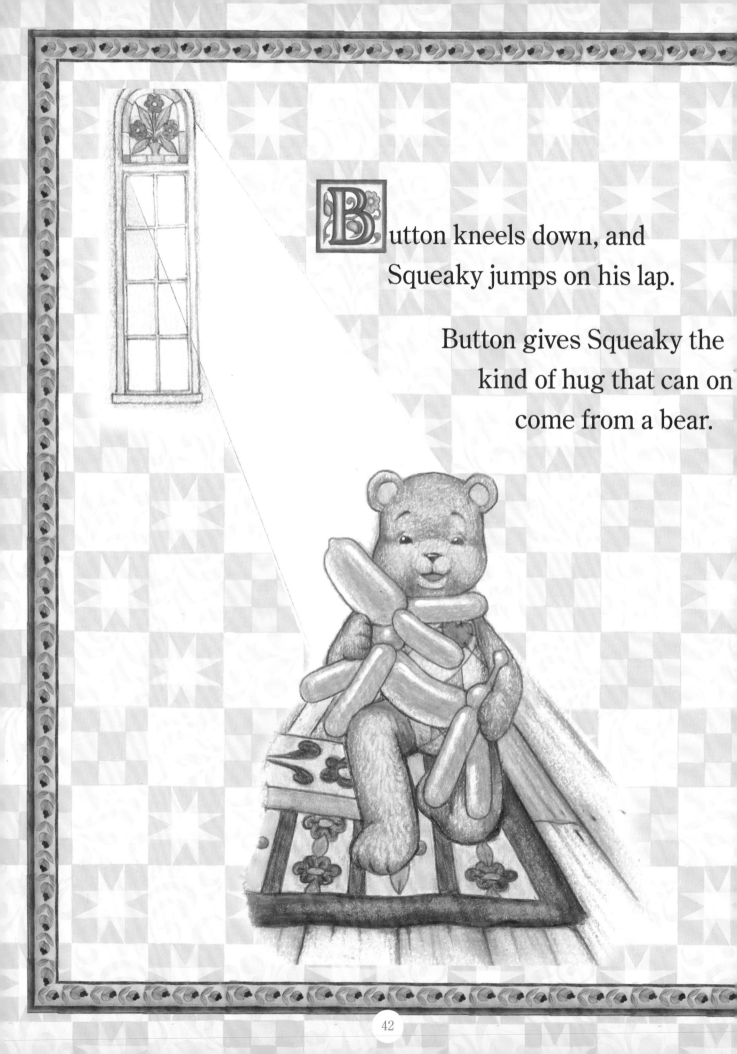

Button kneels down, and
Squeaky jumps on his lap.

Button gives Squeaky the
kind of hug that can on
come from a bear.

queaky says, "That was quite a hug! Good thing I don't pop easily!" They both laugh and dance around the room, then they laugh and dance some more.

Button and Squeaky play for so long that by the end of the day, they're worn out.

Button gathers some old quilts and pillows. They make a cuddly place to sleep, a cozy end to the dreary, drizzly day.

Button and Squeaky snuggle together.

"Good night, Squeaky."

"Good night, Button."

weet dreams!

The End

ISBN 978-1-64124-064-2

Library of Congress Control Number: 2020933548

To learn more about the other great books from Fox Chapel Publishing, or to find a retailer near you, call toll-free 800-457-9112 or visit us at *www.FoxChapelPublishing.com*.

We are always looking for talented authors. To submit an idea, please send a brief inquiry to acquisitions@foxchapelpublishing.com.

Fox Chapel Publishing makes every effort to use environmentally friendly paper for printing.

Printed in China
First printing